You'll Soon Grow Alex

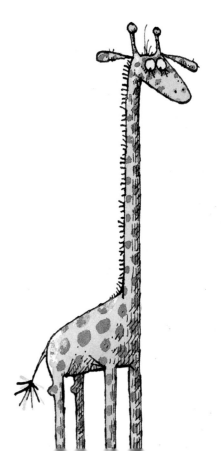

ORCHARD BOOKS
96 Leonard Street, London EC2A 4XD
Orchard Books Australia
Unit 31/56 O'Riordan Street, Alexandria, NSW 2015
ISBN 1 86039 928 2 hardback
ISBN 1 84121 606 2 paperback
First published in Great Britain in 2000
Text © Andrea Shavick 2000
Illustrations © Russell Ayto 2000
The right of Andrea Shavick to be
identified as the author and Russell Ayto
as the illustrator of this work has been
asserted by them in accordance with the
Copyright, Designs and Patents Act, 1988.
A CIP catalogue record for this book is
available from the British Library.
1 2 3 4 5 6 7 8 9 10 hardback
1 2 3 4 5 6 7 8 9 10 paperback
Printed in Singapore

You'll Soon Grow Alex

Andrea Shavick

Illustrated by Russell Ayto

 ORCHARD BOOKS

For three very tall uncles:
Jeremy, Dan and Piggy
A.S.

For Rebecca, Edward and Hannah
R.A.
(In conjunction with Bloxham Playgroup Promises Auction 1999)

Alex was a little boy.

He was so little the other children at school called him 'Shorty'.

He was so little his big sister's friends were always patting him on the head and saying, "Aaahh, isn't he sweet."

Alex didn't like being little.
It made him very unhappy.
How he wished
he was tall.

He couldn't stop thinking about it. He even dreamed about it.

"Mum, how can I grow taller?" asked Alex.

"Protein," said Mum. "About time you had a decent meal. Then you'll soon grow, Alex."

So for three whole weeks Alex ate fish and
eggs and chicken and cheese and baked beans.
And he drank eight glasses of milk a day
with Mum's added Protein Mixture in it.

But it didn't work.

He wasn't any taller.

"Dad, how can I grow taller?" asked Alex.

"Exercise," said Dad. "Lots of exercise and stretching. That should do it. Then you'll soon grow, Alex."

So for three whole
weeks Alex ran
round the garden
every day, and
skipped and jumped.
And Dad made him
a special stretching
machine and Alex
used it every
morning before
he went to school.

But it didn't
work. He wasn't
any taller.

"Emma, how
can I grow taller?"
Alex asked his
big sister.

"Sleep," she said.
"Lots and lots of
sleep. Then you'll
soon grow, Alex."

So for three
whole weeks
whenever it was
time for bed, Alex
went straightaway
without making
any fuss at all.

But it didn't work. He wasn't any taller.
"Mrs Green, how can I grow taller?"
Alex asked his teacher.
"Reading," said Mrs Green.
"Lots of reading and
counting. That should
do it. Then you'll
soon grow, Alex."

So Alex read every book in the school.
And he counted. He counted his
fingers and toes, and stairs
and bears and pears.
His Mum and Dad and
Mrs Green were very
proud of him. "Isn't he
a clever boy," they said.

But it didn't work. He still wasn't any taller. And he was still not happy. Then Alex had an idea. "I know," said Alex. "I'll ask Uncle Danny."

Now Uncle Danny was tall.
Very tall. The tallest person
Alex knew.

"So you want to grow,"
said Uncle Danny.

"Yes, please," said Alex.

"Well, first I'd better tell you
what it's like up here," said
Uncle Danny. "Come with me."

"First of all, when you're tall, you can't fit into a car without being squashed up," said Uncle Danny. "Oh," said Alex. So that was why Uncle Danny couldn't drive in a straight line.

"And then you have to remember to bend down every time you go through a door," said Uncle Danny.

"Oh," said Alex. So that was why Uncle Danny had a lumpy forehead.

"And then it's not easy to find clothes that fit properly," said Uncle Danny.

"Oh," said Alex. So that was why Uncle Danny wore short trousers in the middle of winter.

"Perhaps being as tall as you isn't such a good idea," said Alex. "But I still wish I wasn't so little."

"You're not little. I'll let you into a secret," said Uncle Danny. "You don't want to grow on the outside, no! You need to grow a bit on the inside."

"What do you mean?" asked Alex.

"Listen closely," said Uncle Danny. And he bent right down and whispered in Alex's ear.

From then on, Alex
did all the things Uncle
Danny told him to do.
Like giving his Mum
and Dad and big sister
a hug every morning.

And eating an
ice lolly in the
bath with a
million bubbles
every evening.

And breaking the sound
barrier on his bike.

And making
the ceiling wet
whenever he
went swimming.

And telling the
other children at
school one of
Uncle Danny's
jokes every day.

And smiling at himself
a lot in the mirror.
And do you know
what? It worked.
Alex stopped being
the littlest boy, and
turned into . . .

the happiest

one instead!

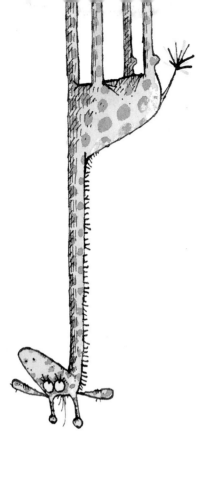